Kinds of Families

By Jenna Lee Gleisner

SPARKS

Picture Glossary

big　　　　　6

silly　　　　12

small 4

tall 8

This family is small.

small

This family is big.

big

This family is tall.

tall

This family is short.

short

This family is silly.

This family is mine.

Do You Know?

This family is _____.

small	big	short
tall	silly	mine